Hunter's Mark

A Beyond Fairytales Story

By
V.S. Morgan

Copyright © 2016 by V.S. Morgan
ISBN: 978-1-68361-091-5
Cover art by Syneca Featherstone

Published by Decadent Publishing Company, LLC
Look for us online at:
www.decadentpublishing.com

Dedication

To Ben, my wonderful son and plot bunny sounding board. Thank you to Joan and my Short in Six sisters for all your support.

Prologue

"Gather round, my friends! Place a few coins in my hat there, for I have a story for you!" Nicodemus called to the people passing by with their corn dogs, cotton candy, and carnival prizes. The lights from the rides and the booths lit up the night sky, and the muted sounds of delighted screams and laughter filled the late summer air.

The storyteller, as old as the hills with his wrinkled face and gray bramble bush of a beard, sat upon a small wooden stool. His eyes sparkled with the knowledge of the ages. His beard rustled, and an electric-blue tarantula emerged, waving its hairy arms as if in greeting before settling on the wizened man's bony shoulder.

Coins jangled into the hat, and a small crowd settled on the grass around the old imp. They quieted as he raised a gnarled hand to get their attention.

"Once upon a time, there was a young shifter. Desperate to feed his poor family, he stole motor vehicles.

"The authorities apprehended the boy one day,

and he had to choose between going to prison and joining the military. Knowing his wolf would die in confinement, he enlisted in the Marine Corps, where he learned many skills. He was an exceptional marksman, for his bullet never missed its target.

"After serving with human soldiers in faraway lands, the young shifter wanted to do something different. Along came a man who offered him a new job, a hunter to seek out and kill the most horrible of mankind.

"For many years, the hunter sought and killed his prey with a clear conscience, for they were indeed the foulest of men. Until, one day, he discovered a mark unlike any other...."

Chapter One

The assassin parked the non-descript car a few houses back from the address Ops had provided.

Thumbing the touchpad at the side of his smart shades, Hunter displayed the picture of his latest target. He grunted in disgust at the grainy quality of the image. What amateur had taken it? Even the shittiest phones could do a hundred times better than this.

Time to check in with his handler.

"Call Rex," he said to his shades, which made Google Glass look like a Cracker Jack prize.

"What up, my man?"

"At the target's residence. Recon begins."

"Roger that," Rex responded.

He ended the connection and ran a hand over his close-cropped hair. Hunter stared at the tiny house. While all the other houses in this hood were downright trashy with jungles for lawns, the place he surveyed was clean and well cared for. Hell, there were even flowers growing in pots, and a wind chime hung from the eaves of the porch. Someone had kept the yard clear of junk and had mowed it trim and tight.

His targets were always the sickest pieces of shit this world had to offer. Murderers, human traffickers, drug lords—the list was long. And none of them had lived in a pad done up all Martha fuckin' Stewart.

This is why he insisted on doing recon. He had no problem killing dirtbags, but it wasn't his style to go in guns blazing. He had forty-eight hours to smoke this guy, and the details had been surprisingly thin. Name, age, and address. No background. Oh, yeah, and a cool two million for a successful hit. With his share of the cut, Mikaela could get that surgery, and he could retire to wherever the hell assassins go...maybe somewhere warm.

A minivan drove by and parked in front of the target's house.

"Run Oregon license plate Charley Delta Alpha five-three-seven," he said.

A plump white lady in a purple cotton top and yoga pants got out and approached the house.

His optic display showed the car belonged to Helena Reynolds, age fifty-five. He pulled up her details. A university faculty member, she volunteered at a local community center, which ran both a soup kitchen and food pantry.

He switched off the visual while she rang the doorbell. His entire body went into "go" mode as the front door opened. In full HD clarity, Casey Smith appeared younger than the twenty-four years listed. What the fuck could someone this young have done to warrant a two million dollar price on his head?

The target carried a large cardboard box overflowing with vegetables to the minivan while the lady talked nonstop at him. He appeared healthy and clean, but his clothes were cheap and worn. He wore a holey, rainbow tie-dyed T-shirt and baggy olive-green cargo shorts.

Casey didn't respond to the woman's chipmunk-speed chatter, just gave her an easygoing smile before placing the box in the back of her vehicle. She patted his arm and climbed into her rig. When she drove away, he leaned down to brush at a spot of dirt on one of his reddened knees.

Heat scorched through Hunter like a match to gasoline. An image flashed in his head of the mark on his knees, licking his lips as he unbuttoned Hunter's shorts, pulling them down to reveal his thick, fully erect member. His cock jerked to attention, completely on board with his wayward thoughts. His wolf grumbled in approval.

He shook his head. What the fuck? He'd never gotten turned on by one of his targets before. Mostly because they were all kinds of fucked up, but shit, it just wasn't professional. He gave his willful dick a thump and told his wolf to go back to sleep.

Casey had returned to the house but soon exited, lugging the crappiest bike he'd ever seen.

Hunter put the car in gear and trailed behind his mark who pedaled down the road with one hand gripping the handlebars and the other clutching a tiny spray of flowers. All while wearing flimsy flip flops—just stupid.

He glanced down at his own outfit and grimaced. Not like he could judge. His job required his blending in, and he donned the clothes necessary to accomplish this. Designer suits, jeans, leathers, tuxedos; you name it. But he'd never looked like a

Bob Marley reject before—black wife beater with a rainbow peace-sign decal, frayed jean cutoffs, and an ancient pair of Birkenstocks. Fucking Birkenstocks! What self-respecting badass wore such wack kicks? James Bond? Hell, no! And he'd absolutely refused to wear the socks Ops packed with the sandals. A brother could only take so much.

The morning sun glinted off Casey's windblown hair as he rode. He had never seen hair that color on a guy before, golden blond with a hint of red. Something white and fluffy stuck out from his backpack. He flipped up his shades and narrowed his eyes. *Hold up, is that a dog?*

He shadowed his target to a small, rundown cemetery.

Casey placed the flowers on the grave. They were inexpensive carnations he'd bought at the grocery store. He wished he could afford a large, beautiful bouquet from a floral shop, but he was almost broke. He smiled. Maggie would have loved the flowers, no matter how cheap they were. She'd raised him alone, and while they'd never had much, he'd never been hungry or neglected. Most importantly, he'd been loved.

Touching the small, flat metal marker, he whispered, "I miss you, Maggie."

Had a year already passed? She had raised him to be strong and confident, but sometimes he felt adrift without his anchor. His adopted mother had been everything to him.

A small whine hauled him out of his thoughts. Priss waved a paw at him. He smiled and bent down to pet the Pomeranian.

"Ready to go, boy?"

The dog yipped in response, and Casey picked him up, placing him in the backpack Priss inhabited during bike rides. After zipping the bag to secure Priss and still allow him to poke his head out and look around, he shouldered the pack before mounting his bike.

Time to set up for Market.

Maggie had been an amazing artist and had taught him everything she knew about pottery. He'd grown up surrounded by art. When he was little, he'd played in the corner of her small booth at the Eugene Saturday Market and began assisting her with customers at the ripe old age of six. Soon, he'd added his own pieces to the displays.

He biked downtown to Eighth and Oak. He greeted other vendors as he made his way to his assigned booth location, which he shared with Glenn, another potter. Partnering up meant they only had to pay one annual membership fee, and they split the rental costs of their eight-by-eight space.

He worked the Market at the Park Blocks every Saturday, April through November, rain or shine. During breaks, he went exploring, checking out all the awesome booths and connecting with other artists.

Glenn had already begun unloading their booth structure from the back of his beat-up van.

"Morning." He grinned at his partner, stepping up to grab the other end.

"Hey, man."

Although about the same age, they were like night and day. While he was a solid five-nine, with a boyish face and reddish-blond hair, Glenn was a spindly six-two with the pallor and jet-black hair typical of goth types. Their temperaments were just as different, but they made a great team.

They set up the thin yet sturdy wooden frame and attached the canvas covering. Then they positioned the display tables and shelves. Casey grabbed their canvas chairs.

They took turns hauling boxes of their work out of the van. He unwrapped and placed the pieces on the display surfaces while Glenn moved the van to the parking lot reserved for vendors.

"Hope we get a better turnout today," Glenn said.

Casey nodded. It'd rained heavily the last two weekends, and not many people had ventured out. Fortunately, he had a few life-drawing modeling sessions lined up at the University of Oregon to supplement his income. He could make that money go far. Besides, the sky was clear and the sun was shining. *Should make some great sales today.*

Chapter Two

Hunter circled the park a few times and snagged a prime parking spot nearby rather than using the free lot a block and a half down. He always kept his exit options close.

With a resigned sigh, he slipped on the ridiculous beanie that completed his fucktastic outfit. His clothes were on the skimpy side, so he concealed his Glock in one of those environmentally friendly cloth bags.

He exited the car and punched in the override code on the digital parking meter, allowing him to set the paid time to eight hours. *Thank you, Ops.*

It didn't take long to relocate his target with the distinctive hair. With his shifter abilities, he didn't need binoculars or any other nonsense. Nope, just the eyes he was blessed or cursed with, depending on his mood.

Dude did indeed have a dog, a fluffy little thing looking like a walking cotton ball. *Crazy.*

He remained near the street and called up info on the park via his shades. Eugene Saturday Market, an outdoor market free to the public. Handcrafted stuff, live music and entertainment, and food. It opened at ten, which gave him an hour to kill. He noticed people hanging out, lounging on the grass around the perimeter, so he found a spot and sat with his back against a tree so he could keep an eye on his objective.

There were lots of places someone of his skillset could hide out—on the roofs of the surrounding buildings, in one of the numerous large trees in the park, in the booths, and eventually in the crowd. His wolf paced uneasily. Neither of them liked crowds.

He surveyed the goth hanging with Casey in the booth. He zoomed in the camera feature of his sunglasses and took a picture.

"Initiate facial recognition."

So far, this assignment wasn't even remotely typical. His marks didn't give away food, visit cemeteries, or work at arts and crafts fairs in shoebox-sized booths. What could he be hiding?

He searched the usual social media sites, but no Casey. Facial rec named Goth Dude as Glenn Anderson. He scanned his details but didn't find anything interesting. However, Glenn posted all over social media. He seemed to have a thing for taking selfies. Hunter rolled his eyes then narrowed them as he studied a recent pic posted on Glenn's Facebook page. A glimpse of a lightly tanned torso with banging tight muscles and sculpted abs, a crescent-moon birthmark on one pec, appeared in the background. His target? His wolf, the fucking slut, wanted to find out.

Once the Market opened, he moved around the park, maintaining a large distance from his target.

What a trippy place, like a time warp right back

to the 1960s. He certainly fit in with the large number of Woodstock wannabes who milled around with gawking tourists. There was wild stuff on display— tie-dyed toilet paper, art made from recycled stuff, and funky-ass mugs with bloody vampire mouths. As he passed a stand with tiny ceramic dragons, he thought about his little sis. Mikaela would love this place.

He watched Casey leave his booth. After taking his dog off to do its business, the mark sat near the fountain and ate his lunch with the mutt curled up at his feet. Signs were posted all over stating no dogs were allowed. It wore a tiny red patch on its collar. A service dog? Weird. He thought only larger dogs were used, and why would his target need one?

Hunter rubbed his temples. Too many damned people here. The heavy scent of burning incense overpowered his nose, and his wolf whined for more food. Eight shish kabobs and a big-ass burrito had barely put a dent in his hunger. He gave in and bought the Pad Thai that had received rave online reviews but longed for a huge, rare steak. Fish, veggies, tofu...*belch.* How did these people survive?

His wolf satisfied, he continued observing. Casey finished lunch and returned to his booth. He smiled and talked with customers as a gentle breeze ruffled his gleaming hair. Damn, that almost sounded poetic. Hunter grimaced. He needed to fucking chill that shit out. He called Rex to check in.

"Yo, dawg, what gives? You pop him already?"

"Negative, too many civilians, and something's not adding up. Target's young, and none of his actions have justified icing him."

"Maybe he's a banger. They grow 'em young,"

Rex said.

"Haven't seen many bangers with little froufrou dogs, working in some tiny-ass booth, happy as can be. Shit, even his hair is happy."

"Even his hair is…? You haven't been eating those 'special brownies' they make there in Eugene, have you?"

"Step off, dickhead. You know I don't do that kind of shit."

"Just fucking with you. Can you smell him?"

"No, too many scents mixing together. I'll need to get closer."

Evil didn't have a smell exactly, but he could pick up hints of it from humans; the stench of fear and violence clung to them long after their crimes were committed.

Glenn left the booth, leaving the mark alone. *Excellent*. Activating the video feed in his sunglasses so his handler could see as well, Hunter ambled over to the neighboring booth, which happened to have the trippy tie-dyed TP.

"I'm buying some for you," he said to Rex.

"Rage on, dude. You totally need to get one of those vamp mugs from the next table for Den Mother. He'll shit a brick!"

He stepped closer to Casey's stall but stumbled over something small and furry. The toe of one Birkenstock caught on a clump of grass as he attempted not to trample the little beast, and he ass-planted with said beast jumping onto his chest to give him a broad doggie smile.

His buddy laughed piss-your-pants-hard in his ear. *Fuck a duck.*

"Miss Priscilla!"

The target he'd worked so hard to observe remotely sank to the ground between his sprawled-out legs, peeling the tiny hairball off his chest and setting it on the ground.

"I'm so sorry! Are you okay?"

Big blue eyes fringed with long, pale lashes scanned his body while strong yet gentle hands moved over his ankles and legs, searching for an injury. Oh, a toucher. His wolf basked in the tactile attention. His breath hitched as those hands glided past his knees and skimmed his thighs.

His dick went from zero to sixty in two seconds. Damn, he needed to get laid after this assignment.

"Oh, my, what a li'l sweetie. Look at those freckles! I wonder if he's got them everywhere. I'd like to lick them," Rex crowed in his ear.

He growled.

The other man chortled. "Possessive, much?"

He inhaled deeply, only to be slammed with the force of a Mack truck. Strawberries on a warm summer's day and fresh-cut grass—shit, his target smelled delicious. He took another breath, and his brain reeled. He's a wolf shifter, too? *Fuck.*

Casey's brows furrowed. "Where are you hurt?"

He forced a smile. "I'm fine. No worries."

His mark returned the smile, his wide and high beam combined with sparkling eyes. Hunter stared, warmth wrapping around him like a blanket. He had no ammo against such a happy, open expression. The guy fucking glowed.

"Here, let me help you up." His prey stood and reached out a hand.

A spark of energy surged up his arm as their hands clasped. His wolf whined in longing. *Down, boy.*

The smaller man gasped, his heated gaze roaming over his body. Hunter's nostrils flared at the scent of Casey's arousal and stifled a groan. *Not helping.*

He just needed to play it cool. After brushing the seat of his shorts, he leaned down and grabbed his bag. Giving him a slight wave, he strolled a short distance away.

What a complete clusterfuck. They didn't hunt shifters. It was bad juju getting involved with pack business.

"Rex, he's a shifter."

"Confirm, did you say shifter?"

"Fuck yes."

"Contacting Den Mother," his handler replied, all business now.

The dog started barking, and he turned. A car jumped the curb, barreling toward the back of the pottery stand.

He darted over and shoved the little wolf out of the way moments before the car plowed through it. The peaceful vibe of the place shattered with the sounds of pottery smashing and people screaming. The scent of fear overpowered even the strongest incense.

Hunter shielded him with his body as the car careened through a few more stands and back onto the street before speeding off. *Fucking A.*

"Priss!"

The dog who had been right at his feet barked. Scooping it up, he stuffed the mutt into Casey's arms and dragged him out of the area.

This couldn't have been an accident, too much of

a coincidence. Someone hadn't honored the forty-eight hour contract and was gunning for the young wolf now. He refused to let that happen.

"Rex, I'm initiating princess protocol."

"Fuck, yeah. Drive to Portland. I'll meet you there."

"Come on, it's time to go." He slung his arm around his mark's shoulder and hauled him to his car.

"Wait, what? I don't know you. Where's Glenn?" His blue eyes darkened with fear, and he twisted his body, attempting to escape. Regret tugged at Hunter for scaring him, but he tightened his hold. He needed to keep the pup alive.

"It's not safe for you here." He reached into the car for his emergency kit.

While the smaller man craned his head around, Hunter stuck him with a hypo, and he went out like a light.

He got both man and his mutt into the backseat without issue then drove toward the river and parked in an abandoned lot. Peering over his shoulder, he saw the dog lick its owner's still cheek.

"Want a treat?" He offered it a piece of Slim Jim. The pooch gave him a "fuck you" look and growled. Not so friendly now.

He raised his shades and allowed his eyes to shift, his wolf staring down the puff ball. It quivered but didn't yield. He growled long and low, and the dog barked at him before flashing tiny white teeth. *Ballsy little thing.* His wolf decided to take a different tack and whined. The pooch moved and let him search the smaller man's clothing.

As he rummaged in his target's pockets, the

waistband of his shorts gaped. His eyebrows shot up at the yellow smiley faces on Casey's boxers. *Un-freaking-believable.*

No ID, but he found a couple of bucks and a cheap phone, one of those burner types that couldn't be traced. He tossed it out the window and ran over it anyway.

As he headed to Portland, he reported in.

"Den Mother, what the hell is going on? Who is this guy?"

"Very good question. It appears Casey Smith doesn't exist. No birth certificate, Social Security number, driver's license, school records, medical records, library card...nothing."

He frowned. "He's been off the grid his entire life? How is that possible? What about the house?"

"It's a rental with no contract on file. Probably pays in cash."

"Any info on the car?"

"Flagged as stolen and found abandoned a few miles out of town. Garrett and Ryland said it smelled of human. They're interrogating his friend now. I've sent out rumors to the media of Casey's death to buy us some time."

Hunter yanked the beanie off his head and flung it onto the passenger seat. "So, what are we going to do with him?"

"The fact he's a shifter complicates things. We'll have to be careful digging around, or the Pack Council will be alerted. Talk to him and see what you learn."

"I drugged and kidnapped him. How likely is he going to be to talk to me?"

"You saved his life, a life he can't return to. He

doesn't have much of a choice."

Chapter Three

Hunter drove into the large garage bay. The "safe house" was actually a warehouse fortified like Fort Knox, with the latest security and surveillance systems. Den Mother didn't fuck around with his assets' safety. His handler stood near the interior entrance. Although a few inches shorter and leaner than him, the man was a good-looking guy. His dark hair and olive skin indicated a Latin or Greek heritage, but he'd never asked. He didn't even know Rex's real name. They closely guarded personal information in their world, even from fuck buddies. Only Akio knew his true identity.

His friend whistled. "Nice legs. And Birkenstocks...you've never looked sexier, dude."

"Shut up and help me with the mutt, yeah?"

"You bagged a princess and a dog, too. An epic day for you, indeed." Rex opened the car door. "Here doggie doggie. What did he call you again? Oh, yeah, Miss Priscilla."

The dog's ears perked up. She crawled over and let the freaking charmer pick her up. Her tail wagged as he continued to coo.

Hunter hefted the little wolf up over his shoulder. The other man shut the car door and left to take the dog out back. Hunter carried his cargo through the long hallway with metal walls. He punched in the code and entered the living area, which looked like the inside of an ordinary house minus windows and exterior doors. Despite the many bedrooms he could have chosen, he strode to the room he always used. His wolf all but howled in triumph as he placed the unconscious man on his bed. His man in his bed. *What the hell? Damn loco wolf.*

Casey's natural scent overwhelmed him. So fucking dope. He wanted to be the one to lick him all over as his buddy had joked about.

He adjusted the erection caught at an awkward angle in his shorts. Shit, what wasn't awkward about this sitch?

With one last glance at his—fuck—*the* princess, he stalked out of the room.

Rex met him in the hallway, crowding into his space, running his hands down Hunter's torso before palming his bulge.

"Oh, poor man. How about I take care of this for you?" Rex nuzzled against his throat as he continued to massage his erection through the denim.

Repelled, his wolf growled a warning. Hunter stepped back and snagged his wrist, yanking his hand off him. "Not tonight."

The other man's eyebrows rose, and he glanced into the room where Casey lay, his lips pursing. "So that's how it is, huh? Never thought the mighty Hunter would fall for a princess."

He snorted. "Yeah, right. Just not in the mood. Babysitting's not my thing."

Rex gave his crotch a meaningful look. "So, I'll get some dinner ready. Dog's all settled in the living room. Oh, and by the way, Miss Priscilla is a boy."

This day just got weirder and weirder. "What?"

They headed for the kitchen.

"Yeah, color me surprised, too. Maybe it's like that movie where Kate Hudson named the boy dog Sophia something."

"No, you got it all wrong. The dog's name was Crawl. She called Matthew McConaughey's dick Princess Sophia."

"Now that's downright cruel. So, steak?"

"Hells, yeah."

***

Casey woke with a pounding headache, and his mouth tasted like Priss poo. Groaning he held his head and tried to open his eyes. *Fuck.* He managed to squint without his head feeling like a splitting melon. He was lying on a strange bed in an unfamiliar room. A glass of water and a bottle of over-the-counter pain medicine rested on the nightstand. He scooted up, slumping against the headboard. His hand trembled slightly when he reached for the pills.

He took two and gulped down the water, his mouth and throat as parched as the Sahara Desert. How had he gotten here? He racked his throbbing brain and only got flashes. *Car. Fear. Priss!* He sniffed the air and calmed. The concentrated scent of his dog told him Priss had been in the room.

He tried to remember...a big man dragging him

away from the chaos and nothing else. Had he been injured? He gingerly moved his fingers over his head, feeling for a bump. Nothing. Casey inhaled and exhaled, working through the pain.

He caught another scent in the room, much fainter than his and Priss'. Dark and delicious like apple cider, wood smoke, and the hint of rain. Like the guy at the Market....

He had seen the smoking-hot man even before Priss had tripped him. He'd watched him stride to the stall nearby, tall, gorgeous and seriously buff. He moved with the power and grace of a predator. It was subtle, though, and he doubted anyone else noticed. After years of people watching, he tended to be more observant than others.

He hadn't missed the mouthwateringly hard body under his hands. And when the man spoke, his deep voice had hummed through him.

His dick hardened despite the lingering headache. He peered down at his tented shorts. He burned for a man he knew nothing about. A sexy stranger who had saved him from getting squished by a car....

"Ah, the princess is awake! Come, have some breakfast." A handsome dark-haired guy stood at the door way. Priss nestled in his beefy arms.

He didn't smell as good as the other man but shared a similar, subtle undertone.

"I'm Rex, by the way. Friend of the big guy who saved you." His smile was easy and friendly.

So many questions to ask and out popped, "Why'd you call me a princess?"

"Well, when we rescue someone, we call them a princess."

"Even men? You don't call them princes?"

"Nope."

He snorted. "Yeah, cuz that would be stupid."

"Says the guy with a boy dog named Miss Priscilla," Rex said with a smirk.

"Touché." He climbed off the bed and followed him out of the room. Priss gave a happy yip as the big guy handed him over. Casey buried his face into soft fur, the contact with his dog bringing the peace he needed.

They entered a large living room, which was a cross between the bat cave and a man cave, with its high tech equipment, huge wall-mounted screens, and high-end yet comfortable looking overstuffed chairs and sectional couches.

"So, tell me the story behind his name. I'm dying to know."

"I found him as a stray. He was so dirty, I couldn't even tell what color he was. When I got him all washed and dried, he pranced around with a strut. I laughed and called him a Miss Priss. The name stuck. I call him Miss Priscilla when he's been really naughty."

Rex chuckled. "Like tripping Hunter. Fucking hilarious, by the way."

Weird. He said it like he'd been there, but maybe he had. He couldn't remember shit. Wait...his mysterious rescuer's name was Hunter.

"Where is he?" He needed answers.

"Just got back from a long run, so he's taking a shower. He had some extra energy to burn." He winked and slapped Casey on the shoulder. Must be some inside joke.

He followed the other man into the ultra-modern

kitchen. The stainless-steel appliances actually matched, unlike in his little kitchenette. Instead of the chipped laminate counters he was used to, black granite gleamed. *Whoa.* Rex opened the fridge. "So, what do you want to eat? We've got sausage, bacon, eggs—"

"I'm a vegetarian." He gave an inward sigh of longing.

The guy looked at him like he'd grown a second head, but Casey continued his long-used lie.

"I have epilepsy. Certain foods, including animal protein, trigger my seizures."

"No shit. I've never heard of a.... Well, never mind. I think there's some green stuff in the fridge."

The only green stuff he found lived on a lump of moldy cheese, so he settled for wheat toast and orange juice. The smell of cooking meat made him fidgety, but he couldn't risk eating any. Not after last time. He sat down at the black rectangular table, which was a far cry from his little card table. But as nice as this place was, it wasn't home.

The strong scent of apple cider and wood smoke washed over him as the man from the Market strode through the living room and entered the kitchen wearing a fitted black T-shirt and jeans that clung to his thick thighs and tight ass. He had the sudden urge to bite that ass. Damn it, he hadn't even touched meat, and he was getting all wolfy. He needed to focus, or he'd end up in some lab somewhere, getting experimented on with probes and stuff.

Without the shades, the man's eyes were intimidating. He picked at his toast to avoid the piercing dark-chocolate gaze. He was glad to be sitting because his knees were like jelly.

The big kitchen seemed to shrink as the large men worked together preparing their breakfast. Rex manned the gas stove, heating up a skillet. Hunter chopped ham to go into their omelets. Although there was tons of counter space, they remained in each other's personal space, weaving around each other with ease. It was clear they knew each other well. He didn't want to think about how well. Instead, he wanted to brand Hunter as his. To climb him like a tree and kiss those big, full lips and nibble along the pencil-thin beard that accentuated his strong jaw. He wanted to be the only one to touch, taste, and lick his smooth, espresso-hued skin.

"Casey here's a vegetarian. Says meat makes him have seizures." Rex waved a spatula at him.

He nodded and sipped his juice. "When can I go home?"

Hunter's lips tightened to a flat line. "You can't. Someone tried to kill you."

"How do you know it wasn't just an accident?"

"Because there's a price out on your head." Rex slid an omelet onto the other man's plate.

A scrap of memory flashed. The sharp prick to his arm...his pounding headache. He'd been drugged. A spike of fear slammed through him. Priss yipped and pawed at his leg. He leaned over and picked him up. He stroked his fur while assessing the two men, but their impassive expressions revealed nothing.

"You were sent to kill me."

"Yes," Hunter said, taking a seat on the opposite side of the table.

The brutal honesty of the answer quieted his racing mind. He grasped the edge of the table. *Steady.* "But you didn't, despite having the time and the means. Why?"

His would-be assassin's eyes bore into him. "I ice bottom feeders. That isn't you. But someone doesn't have the same moral boundaries I do."

"Are you with the government?" So, they didn't want to kill him, but that didn't mean they wouldn't turn him over to some creepy scientists....

"No, we work for a private organization." The baritone voice soothed his jangled nerves.

Rex gave him a sympathetic look as he sat down next to his friend. "We're not going to hurt you, Casey. We want to help."

"What about my partner Glenn?"

Hunter glowered, his fork paused halfway to his mouth. "Partner?"

Was he homophobic or jealous? He hoped jealous. Jeez, he had a death wish. "My business partner. Is he okay?"

"Some of our associates have him at a secure location," Rex said and began to eat.

"Do you know anyone who would want to hurt you?"

"No."

Hunter pulled out his phone. "What do you know about this? He held it out so Casey could see.

He watched a blurry video of a large, pale wolf running down a street. Could it be? It'd been posted a year ago. *Damn it*.

"Your *partner* posted this video and exchanged e-mails with someone very interested in the wolf since they aren't common in your part of Oregon." Hunter paused. "They talked about other things, too, like you and your distinctive birthmark." He set the phone down with a thunk.

A shiver ran down Casey's spine.

"Have you ever heard of people changing into animals?" Rex asked.

Damn it, he sucked at lying, but he had to try. He widened his eyes and assumed his most innocent expression. "Like werewolves? There's a storyteller that visits the Market. Nicodemus tells some crazy cool stories."

"Can you shift?" Hunter persisted.

His heart pounded. They were too close to the truth.

"It's okay, we're shifters, too." Rex picked up their now-empty plates and carried them to the counter.

"I don't know what the hell you're talking about." He crossed his arms over his chest.

"I can smell you, Little Wolf. Your fear. Your lies," Hunter said in a hard tone. Damn, his deep voice turned him on. *Can he smell that, too?*

The other man's nostrils flared, and the corner of his mouth kicked up. Casey flushed.

"I don't believe you."

Hunter pushed back from the table and stood. He straightened to his full height, his shoulders back and his legs braced. His eyes bored into Casey. It took everything in him not to squirm under his gaze. The hit man cocked his chin up, and a muscle jerked in his jaw. Jesus, had he pushed him too far? The large man grasped the bottom of his T-shirt and yanked it up over his head, revealing a wall of hard, dark muscle which rippled as he flung the shirt on the floor. Casey's eyes widened when he stripped off his jeans as well.

Holy hell, he goes commando. He had a huge

dick, impressive even when flaccid. Casey licked his lips, fear and arousal warring inside him.

Hunter arched an eyebrow before his body shimmered and a large black wolf stood in his place. Priss jumped off his lap and danced up to the wolf, flipping over and presenting his belly. He sniffed at Priss then stalked toward Casey who leaped out of his chair and backed into a corner. The shifter burrowed against him.

"Is he going to eat me?" He flicked a glance at Rex, who leaned against the counter like it was an everyday occurrence to have a huge wolf in the kitchen.

The other man laughed. "I'm sure he'd love to devour you. Just not in the way you're thinking."

He pushed the muzzle out of his crotch and held the big face in his hands. He peered into the most soulful brown eyes he'd ever seen. *So beautiful.*

The wolf whined, and Casey scratched his head. He rumbled and licked his cheek.

"See? He likes you," the other man said with a smile.

The wolf Hunter eased away, and soon he reverted to his big, naked, less-hairy self. He hated to see those clothes go back on.

"I've never met anyone like me before." He returned to his chair, and Priss jumped up onto his lap.

"You were raised by humans?" Rex asked.

He nodded. "My family died when I was a baby, and Maggie adopted me. I didn't even know I was different until puberty hit. Maggie taught me how to control myself using diet, meditation, and Priss."

"The dog?" The two men glanced at the ball of

fluff.

"He alerts me when my wolf is too close to the surface and helps keep me calm. I say I have epilepsy so he can go with me everywhere, including the Market." He pointed to the patch on Priss' collar. "This says he's a seizure-assistance dog."

"You keep your wolf in lockdown all the time?" Rex asked.

He nodded. "Yeah, Maggie said it was the only way to stay safe." He tilted his head toward the phone and the frozen image of the wolf still on the screen. "That's me. I was so devastated when she passed, I lost it."

Hunter gripped his shoulder, sympathy warming his dark eyes. "We'll talk to Den Mother and figure out what to do next. In the meantime, you can stop suppressing your wolf. You're safe here."

His stomach rumbled. "Do you have any more bacon?"

Rex grinned. "You bet."

Chapter Four

Hunter paced in the living room as he gave Den Mother a quick update on the little they knew. He was ordered to remain at the safe house with Casey until further notice.

"We'll start searching the shifter databanks as soon as Rex returns to HQ with Casey's DNA sample, but it may take a few days since we can't go through the usual channels. Cyber's still following the e-mail trail, but whoever was communicating with Glenn covered their tracks well," Den Mother said.

Rex went out for supplies, including dog food for Priss, who had been cutting loose some rank gas. *Note to self, never feed a dog a Slim Jim ever, ever again.*

Casey sat on a nearby couch, staring off at nothing. He could almost hear the gears turning in the little wolf's head.

He knew jack shit about comforting people, but he followed his instincts and sat next to him, legs splayed out wide. Priss jumped down and climbed into a chair, curling up to sleep.

"You all right?" he said when smaller man didn't

acknowledge his presence. He reached his arm around him, hauling him up close.

Casey snuggled into his side, draping an arm around his waist. His wolf rumbled in pleasure. This comforting thing wasn't half-bad.

"It's so unreal finding out someone wants me dead. How much did they offer?"

"Two million."

The little wolf jerked back to stare at him. "That's so much money. Why didn't you go through with it?"

"I have two rules. One, I don't kill innocent people. Two, I don't kill shifters."

He brushed his fingers over the dusting of freckles across the bridge of Casey's nose before running them down his smooth cheek and across his stubbled jaw. *So damn cute.*

The other man blinked at him but leaned into his touch. "So you're done, just like that?"

"Just like that." He drew him back against his side.

They were quiet for a while. He stroked Casey's soft hair, breathing in his heady scent. He closed his eyes, the smells taking him back to happier times with his family, a long time ago.

"Can I ask you a question?"

He ran his hand down the smaller man's back. "Depends on the question."

"Is Rex your boyfriend?"

"I wouldn't be holding you like this if he was."

"Good." He smiled at the obvious relief in Little Wolf's voice.

His temperature spiked as Casey nuzzled into his neck, soft lips and prickly stubble brushing against the sensitive skin beneath his ear. He shifted the redhead away from his neck, cradling his face, so pale compared to his own dark hands. His blue eyes were bright, his cheeks flushed as he gazed at his mouth. The little wolf looked like he wanted to eat him up. He'd meant to comfort him, but he inflamed Hunter's darker impulses.

He dipped down and slanted his lips over Casey's. He hummed in pleasure as he responded to his kiss. He pressed with his tongue, seeking entrance, and when he opened his mouth, Hunter delved in. Little Wolf tasted of minty toothpaste and a sweetness that was all his own.

They made out on the couch like teenagers. He couldn't remember when he'd ever taken the time to simply kiss and caress, mapping out a lover's body with his hands and mouth. Nope, he liked to strip, fuck, and move on. But not with Casey. Hell, they still had all their clothes on, and he burned, ready to combust.

Hunter slid his hands under the other man's shirt and explored his silky-smooth back before cupping his choice ass. Casey ground against his thigh. If they kept this up, he would blow in his jeans....

He moaned in protest when the smaller man climbed off the couch. He reached a hand out to him but stopped as he dropped to his knees. The little wolf opened Hunter's jeans, and he lifted his hips so he could pull them down. Casey's hungry stare did all kinds of things for his ego and his wolf. He took a deep breath, resisting the urge to pounce on him. His instincts said have patience and let the young shifter lead this.

Casey licked his cupid's-bow lips, and he

imagined those pretty pink lips stretched wide around his cock. His dick jerked, precum beading from its slit.

He groaned as Little Wolf leaned down and lapped it up. He glanced up, a wicked smile on his face, before he blew air over the tip.

"Fuck! Oh, baby, please." He *never* begged, but he wanted him so bad. Wanted whatever he would give him…. His vision shifted to black and white.

Casey's eyes were still very human, but when his smile broadened, his canines lengthened slightly. *Oh, fuck, so sexy.*

He grasped Hunter's cock and slid his calloused hand up and down as if learning his shape and size. He fought pumping into that firm grip. He watched the reddish-blond head bend to take him in. The little wolf first focused on the tip and then taking more of him, working him with his tongue. Hunter buried his hands in that thick, soft hair. When he tugged on the light-colored strands, the other man groaned.

Little Wolf played him like an instrument, ramping him up to the highest notes only to stop at the brink, edging him to prolong the pleasure. He'd never been so turned on from a blow job in his life. He wondered how much experience Casey had to be so skilled, and his wolf growled at the thought.

The proximity alert beeped, and he flicked his glance to the large monitor mounted on the wall. Rex, the fucking cock blocker.

Wolves weren't prudes. Being naked was natural, and they didn't mind fucking in front of others. But Casey had been raised by humans.

He tapped the younger wolf's head. "Rex's back."

The other man sucked harder, his hands

clenching and unclenching the loose denim around Hunter's thighs. He moaned. Maybe the little shifter was more in touch with his wolf nature than he realized.

"Oh, fuck!"

He opened his eyes. His friend and former fuck buddy leaned against the door jam, an erection straining his jeans. Licking his lips, he kept his gaze locked on the other man, who stroked his own package.

He gasped as sharp teeth grazed his member. He snapped his eyes down to Casey who peered up him, his eyes a hypnotic blue, demanding, without words, his full attention. "I'm here, baby."

The little wolf smiled around his cock before sucking him with renewed energy, and Hunter threw his head back, his orgasm hitting him hard and fast. He yelled, coming in Casey's mouth as stars danced before his eyes. Fucking insane.

The little shifter sat back on his heels, licking his red, swollen lips. His wolf howled at the sexy sight.

He grasped Casey and yanked him up onto his lap. He kissed him, tasting his own salty essence. Hunter blindly fumbled for the waistband of his shorts and shoved them down. He stroked the long, slender cock a few times, and the other man came with a loud moan. The sounds of his pleasure and the smell of his release triggered a possessive instinct Hunter had never experienced before.

He licked cum off his hand, savoring the slightly sweet flavor. Should have known it would taste just as good as the rest of him. Casey watched him, his eyes lust blown. Hunter kissed him again then tucked his head against his neck, his arms wrapped around him. His chest swelled with a foreign sensation. It took his blissed-out brain a few seconds to identify it—complete and utter satisfaction. Little Wolf sighed, a dreamy, contented sound. He closed his eyes and rubbed his jaw against his head, needing his scent on his own skin.

Rex coughed. He had forgotten about him. Casey must have too because he sat up with a start. He blushed bright red but had an adorable wolfish smile on his face.

His friend gave them a pained yet amused look. "Well, if you two are finished, I have prezzies for the princess and his pooch!"

Casey yanked up his shorts and scrambled to stand. His emotions churning, Hunter focused on righting his own pants.

Rex handed the little wolf four bags.

"Wow! Thank you! I'll grab a quick shower," Casey said and left.

"I know I should be pissed off, but that was so fucking hot." His buddy brought in more bags, placing them on the floor.

"Sorry, man. He must be a bit of an exhibitionist," he mused. Angel-faced and kinky, he was all over that.

The other man laughed. "You can be really dense sometimes. He wanted me to see him claiming you. Gotta give it to him, didn't expect such a ballsy move."

The C word made him uneasy, but his own possessive instincts were off the charts. In fact, both he and his wolf were pissed at all the shit Rex had bought him. He should be the one providing for Casey. "You got him a Hugo Boss suit? So, who are you now, the Fairy Fucking Godmother?' He sprang up off the couch and paced.

"Why are you being so bitchy? I'm the one walking around with three legs here." Rex planted his hands on his hips. "He had only the clothes on his back, and Den Mother would have freaked if he'd seen those flip flops. Figured I'd do him up right." His buddy regarded him with a perceptive gleam in his eyes. "Maybe you should have left and let me give the princess a little TLC."

Hunter got up in his grill and glared, his wolf ready to beat Rex's punk ass.

The other man laughed and shoved him back. "Yeah, I thought that'd be your answer. How about you pay for his shit?"

"Damn right, I'm paying for it." Somewhat appeased, he checked out the rest of the bags.

Jesus, Rex had really gone to town at the pet store. He'd bought doggie kibble, food and water dishes, squeaky toys, treats, a brush, and a tiny rhinestone-studded collar.

He held up the collar and raised an eyebrow.

"Little man needs some bling," Rex said with a shrug and snatched it out of his hand.

They both cocked their heads as Casey began singing in the shower. "Happy" by Pharrell Williams, go figure.

"Must be weird being attracted to someone so damn perky. Doesn't it bug you out?"

"No, I think it's...sweet." And fuck if he didn't mean it.

"Wow, I think he blew both your heads."

Hunter gave him the finger, and the other man snickered.

"What does he smell like to you?"

His friend studied him, his brows bunched. "A dude. Barely scented his wolf, it was so faint. I'm surprised you noticed so quickly. Although it's stronger now." Rex picked up Priss and replaced his old collar with the tricked-out one. "Why, what does he smell like to you?"

He couldn't help but smile. Just thinking about Little Wolf's scent made him mellow. "Like summer— sunshine, strawberries, and fresh-cut grass."

Rex's eyes widened. "Fuck, Hunter. I think he might be your mate."

"What? The hell you say!" He clutched his hand around one of Priss' new toys, which emitted a loud squeak. The dog barked, and he chucked the toy to him. He grimaced as the other man grinned like a fucking goon.

"No I mean it. Mates are supposed to smell really yummy to each other."

"Have you ever heard of two male mates?"

"No, but that doesn't mean it isn't possible. Answer me this. What would you do if Casey had sex with someone else?"

A red haze obscured his vision as rage choked him. Kill, he'd kill any motherfucker who touched him.

"Exactly."

Oh, fuck. What am I going to do with a mate?

Clean and in fresh clothes, Casey left the bedroom. When he found Rex alone in the living room, his good mood tanked and his cheeks heated as it fully hit him what he'd done in front of him. He shoved a hand through his hair and cleared his throat. *Awkward.*

"Where's Hunter?"

"Walking the pooch." Rex crouched next to a backpack, slipping in snacks and bottled water.

Casey viewed all the doggie paraphilia strewn on the floor. "Wow, is all that stuff for Priss?"

"Yeah, it was fun shopping for you guys. I also got veggies in the fridge since you're used to vegetarian food." The other man stood and shouldered the pack.

"Thanks for everything. Look—I'm sorry about earlier...."

Rex smirked. "Definitely more entertaining than you peeing on his leg."

He scrunched up his nose. "Gross. I'm not into watersports."

"Keep forgetting you didn't grow up around other wolves. I meant marking your territory," the big guy said with a laugh.

Did I do that? Deep down he knew the answer was yes, and part of him was very pleased, the rest not so much. "I know you and Hunter are...friends. It wasn't cool to rub it in your face."

"No worries. Once those animal instincts kick in, it's hard to rein them in. Tell me something. What does he smell like to you?"

Random, much? "He smells like apple cider, rain, and wood smoke. Reminds me of when Maggie and I went camping. Best memories of my life."

Rex smiled broadly and gave him a side hug. "You take good care of him, princess."

A snarl issued from behind them, and he spun to see Hunter give his friend a kill-you-dead-where-you-stand glare.

Rex chuckled. "That's my cue to go."

Chapter Five

Casey fidgeted in the plush chair, unable to settle despite Priss' presence and the rom com on TV. Normally, he would have enjoyed watching Ryan Reynolds banter with Sandra Bullock, but even Ryan naked couldn't hold his attention. He didn't know what he'd expected after Rex left, but tall, dark, and stony wasn't it. When he had asked where they were, the answer was Portland. And, no, he couldn't take Priss for a walk outside. After that, Hunter didn't say much, grunting at him when he mentioned watching TV. The big guy had an arsenal laid out on the kitchen table, meticulously cleaning and oiling each weapon, although he suspected they were just fine without the attention.

He rubbed the back of his neck and tried to focus on the movie again. He flushed, remembering going down on Hunter. He had loved sucking his big cock. His mouth watered just thinking about it. Had it been good for Hunter? Had he found him lacking compared to...? No, *not* going there. He sensed the weight of the large man's stare on him, not for the first time, yet his gaze was elsewhere when Casey looked his way.

He tugged at his hair in frustration. He normally didn't question things to death like this, but what else could he do cooped up in this place? There weren't even windows! He hated being idle. He worked long hours creating his pottery pieces. In his off time, he tended the garden, volunteered at the community center, or hiked. Being stuck indoors with a grumpy jailer sucked hard and *not* in the good way.

Shaking his head at his melodramatic thoughts, he brushed his hand over Priss' back. Casey's body tingled and twitched, the sensation of ants crawling all over his skin gave him the creeps. His wolf itched to come out. He placed Priss on the floor and bounced out of the chair, earning a quick glance from the other man. He flipped off the TV before powering up the streaming music system Rex had shown him how to use earlier. Music always made him feel better.

He went into the kitchen and began pulling out ingredients for dinner. He liked cooking and picked a labor-intensive dish to pass the time.

Hunter knew enough cooking basics to get by, but Casey seriously schooled him as he prepared homemade lasagna noodles and marinara sauce. Hell, he hadn't even known what a pasta maker looked like.

Little Wolf sang and danced while he worked, lost in his own world. He sure could move for a white boy. He hid a smile, thinking the other were's family must not have had the "no be-bopping in the kitchen" rule that his had. His mom had lightly smacked him upside the head more than once for not following that rule.

When the oven timer dinged, he hungered for both the delicious smelling food and the sizzling cook who'd prepared it. Damn, those new jeans looked so fly, all snug-like on that sick ass—especially when Casey had danced to Jason Derulo's "Talk Dirty." What a fucking tease that had been.

He removed the last of his gear off the table, and his stomach grumbled. Casey plated up a big portion of lasagna with green salad and crisp bread and placed it in front of him without a word. As big of a dick as he had been, he couldn't believe Little Wolf would share with him, let alone serve him.

"Thank you."

"You're welcome." The other man didn't meet his gaze and sat down with his own food.

They ate in silence, the tension between them a living thing. It killed him to see the miserable look on that sweet face and the way he pushed the food around his plate. Casey was so fine. He needed someone so much better than a killer. Yet his gut roiled at the thought of him being with anyone else. *I'm so screwed.*

"This is really good. If fact, it's the best thing I've ever eaten," he said.

Casey's eyes met his, a small smile playing over his face.

Right there, now that's the shit.

"Glad you like it." His expression clouded. "Hunter, are we okay? I mean after earlier...."

Fuck. He closed his eyes and called himself every single nasty name in the book. He should have realized Casey might be feeling uncertain about what they'd shared with him blowing hot and chilly all in the same day. Shit, what if he felt used?

He reached out and clasped the small shifter's free hand, rubbing his thumb over the back of it. "I know things are messed up right now, but we're solid."

Casey squeezed his hand back. "Cool."

***

In the semi-dark of his room, Hunter stared at the ceiling, his head resting on top of his folded arms. He should be out cold because he hadn't slept much in the last forty-eight hours. He moved around the bed, the gazillion thread-count Egyptian cotton sheets as rough as sandpaper on his over-sensitized skin. He and his wolf were restless knowing a mere wall separated them from their potential mate.

He lifted his head. Was that a whine? *Priss*.

He flung the light blanket off and stalked to the next room. He knocked, but the other man didn't respond. Priss barked. *Fuck it*. All his senses on high alert, he opened the door and entered, scanning the room to assess the situation.

The young shifter mumbled and thrashed around on the bed. Priss pawed at him and whined, but Little Wolf didn't wake up. Priss gave him a "fix this, motherfucker" look. Damn, for a prissy little thing, the dog was hardcore.

"Casey, wake up, man. You're having a bad dream." He shook his shoulder.

Nope, didn't help.

He sat down and combed his hand through Casey's hair, and he calmed a bit. Hunter settled into a more comfortable position, his back against the headboard, and continued to stroke his hair. He couldn't get over its softness, so different from his own short, coarse hair. He'd just stay here a while....

Hunter's eyes shot open. At some point during the night, he'd curled around the smaller man with Priss perched on top of his hip like a regular puppy pile. He suppressed a groan at the feel of his erection against a deliciously pert ass. Everything screamed at him to tap that sweet thing. He placed Priss on the bed and rolled onto his back, his engorged dick throbbing. *Fuck.* He looked at his watch. Nine a.m. Shit, how had he slept so late? He glanced over at Casey who looked so fucking adorable with his hair standing on end, his face softened in sleep. He wanted nothing more than to wrap his body around him again, but he needed to check in with Den Mother.

Priss followed him, and he took him outside to do his business once he'd taken care of his own. While the dog ate kibble, he logged into a secure vid line. One of the mounted flat screens blinked once, twice, and displayed Akio Tamashiro, aka Den Mother, who looked the same as the day they'd met ten years ago. Appearing to be in his mid-thirties, only Akio's worldly eyes hinted at his true age of 350. The vampire gave him a small smile.

"Hello, Hunter," he said with the slightest accent. "How are you holding up?"

"Fine. Any news yet?"

"Still waiting on the test results."

He scrunched up his face and huffed out a breath in frustration. He didn't know how long he could be around Casey and not fuck his amazing ass.

"I know this isn't what you do. I'll send someone

in for babysitting duty as soon as we know more."

"No! I mean it's fine. This is my assignment. I'll see it through."

Akio's face remained serene, but he studied him. "If that is what you wish."

He fought the urge to avert his eyes under his boss's scrutiny. "It is. Listen, Casey's going a bit stir crazy. It should be low risk to take him up to Mt. Hood late tonight. Will you clear that?"

"Yes, it would be good for him to get out. Encourage him to shift, as well."

"Will do." He shut down the link and stretched. Little Wolf's scent lingered on his body, causing a low hum of arousal.

He strode to the bathroom and stripped. He set the shower temp to steaming hot and climbed in. Grabbing the body wash, he squirted a large glob into his palm. He rubbed his hands over his chest and down his abs, hardening as he cleaned his dick and balls. Getting another squirt of body wash, he grasped his throbbing cock and stroked. As his dick slid in and out of his tight grip, he remembered the little shifter's mouth sucking him. The sight, the feel of his hot mouth had been pure heaven. It didn't take long for his balls to tighten up, and he ejaculated onto the tile. He rested his forehead against the wall. *Fuck.*

Chapter Six

Casey stretched his arms over his head and yawned. He vaguely remembered some messed-up dreams, but then dreaming about Hunter. He'd woken up in the middle of the night to discover the big guy was indeed there, holding him against his chest. Snuggling in, he'd gone back to sleep.

After a quick stop in the bathroom, he wandered out to the living room.

Hunter glanced up from his tablet. "Sleep good?"

"Yeah. What time is it?" He dragged a hand through his hair, trying to tame it.

"Noon. Thought you were going to snooze the day away."

"Wow, I don't usually sleep that late. You eat lunch yet?"

"Nope."

Casey headed to the kitchen with the large man following him. "Cool. I'll nuke some leftover lasagna."

"Sounds good. I checked in with Den Mother. No news yet about your family. I know it's tough for you being here, so I asked if we could take a field trip."

He stopped rooting around in the fridge and turned to glance at Hunter. "Really?"

"Yeah, Mount Hood National Forest is about twenty miles from here. We can go tonight. Run around and shit." The other man set plates and silverware on the counter.

He grinned and pumped his fist in the air. "Sweet!"

"We'll practice your shifting," Hunter said, as if were the easiest, most natural thing to do.

He frowned, his excitement dimming. "I hope I can do it."

Hunter rubbed Casey's shoulder. "You can, and I'll be there to help you."

***

Casey hopped out of the SUV and breathed in the fresh, pine-scented air. He laughed, thrilled to be outside, especially with his wolf itching to run. He wished Priss could have come, too, but they needed to focus on shifting.

He sprinted up the slope. Finding a clearing, he flung his arms out wide and circled, feeling the breeze through his fingers.

Hunter chuckled. "You nuts, boy, looking like Julie Andrews in *The Sound of Music*."

He laughed and twirled around until he got dizzy and fell to the ground, the scent of moist earth a balm to his soul. He gazed up at the stars, which shone bright in the clear sky. The other man crouched next to him and ruffled his hair. "Get it out of your system. Go hug some trees or something."

He smiled up at him. "This is awesome. Thanks!"

"Welcome, baby."

He tingled all over, staring into Hunter's smoldering eyes. His wolf whimpered with anticipation. Jumping up, he took off at a jog with the big guy close behind. He climbed over a log and then paused to catch a breath.

"Ready to try?" Hunter asked.

"How do you do it?"

"Just focus on your wolf. Imagine being one. Thinking about running helps. And when you're ready to change back, think about your human form."

Casey slipped out of his clothes and clenched his fists. Closing his eyes, he shut out everything except his wolf.

A warm, naked body pressed against his back, and the other man ran his large hands up and down his arms. "Think about your wolf. About how much fun we'll have running together. Come out and play, Little Wolf. My wolf is dying to meet you."

He pictured the black wolf running in the forest with the pale wolf from the video...with him. His wolf rose to the surface.

"Let it go." Hunter leaned down, running his lips over his ear.

He shuddered and surrendered to the wolf.

Standing before Hunter was the most beautiful wolf he'd ever seen, his fur a mix of cream and red. Ice-blue eyes blinked up at him.

"You're gorgeous," he whispered, and wolf Casey gave him a toothy smile before he bounded off.

He shifted and chased after the pale wolf, howling with joy.

They played for hours, exploring the woods,

often stopping to bump into each other and wrestle. After pausing to drink at a stream, the pale shifter shook water on him and raced off. Hunter pursued and tackled him. Casey's wolf whined and tipped his head, exposing his vulnerable neck. The display of sweet submission sent Hunter into sexual overload, and he rolled off the small wolf. Panting, fighting for control, he shifted back to human form.

Little Wolf pounced after him. When he landed on Hunter, he'd shifted to a naked, squirming man, their cocks rubbing together. Casey laughed and ground against him again. He groaned and pulled the other man up for a kiss. Not breaking contact, he reached down and grasped their erections in one hand, jacking them together. The young shifter gasped in his mouth, and their tongues tangled in a hot, moist kiss.

Casey groaned as he climaxed, his cum spurting over his hand and onto his stomach. His own orgasm surged up through him, and he came, adding his release to the mix. Casey collapsed on him, and Hunter kissed his sweaty temple.

"I knew you could do it."

Little Wolf just mumbled and snuggled against his chest.

He chuckled. "Don't go to sleep. We can't stay here. Besides, I've got a pine cone digging into my right butt cheek."

"Okay, but I get first shower."

"Deal."

Casey slept on the way back and didn't make it to the shower, instead crashing on his bed. Hunter cleaned him up with a washcloth. When he rose to leave, strong fingers wrapped around his wrist.

"Stay."

"Okay, Mr. Bossy." He shucked off his clothes and crawled into bed, gathering Casey close. Closing his eyes, he and his wolf sighed. Spooning was the best thing ever.

Chapter Seven

His father was alive. His DNA connected him to Aleksander Pawlak, Alpha of one of the most powerful packs in the Midwest, according to Hunter. Casey stared at the image of the older man on the living room monitor. Commanding leader, yeah, he could believe it. He looked like one cold-ass bastard. He thrust his hands in his pockets and rocked back on his heels. "What about my mother?"

Hunter shot him a sympathetic look from the couch. "She died in a house fire. It was initially reported your entire family perished. Your father was badly burned, and if he'd been human, he would have died."

He glanced at the picture again. "But he doesn't have any scars."

"Shifters have incredible healing abilities."

"How did I end up alive and in Oregon?"

"They're still exploring that."

"So what's next?" Casey flopped down onto the couch next to the big man.

"We're flying to Minnesota. There's a pack

summit in Minneapolis. Den Mother's setting up a meeting with Pawlak, so we'll be on neutral ground." Hunter's muscles bunched and tension radiated off him as he rolled his shoulders.

He rested his hand on the other man's arm. "You don't have to go."

"No, it's all right. I just get edgy around other wolves."

"What's your pack like?"

A muscle in Hunter's jaw jerked. "I don't have a pack anymore."

"Is it because you're gay?"

The large shifter shook his head. "No. Weres don't get diseases or have many of the health issues humans do, but sometimes we have problems." He paused, pursing his lips. "My little sister was born with a deformity, restricting her to a wheelchair. It also prevents her from shifting. The pack wanted my parents to abandon her in the forest."

"What!" Bile rise in his throat.

Hunter nodded. "They refused and were banished. My dad worked as a mechanic at shop run by humans. Money was tight, but things were good until he died."

"How did he die?"

"Thugs tried to rob the place. They shot and killed him."

"God, that's awful." He rubbed Hunter's leg above his knee.

"I was the man of the house after that but had trouble finding legit jobs. I started boosting cars for chop shops just so my mom and sister could eat."

"What happened?"

"I got caught and ended up in the military for a

number of years until I met Den Mother."

"Are you still in contact with your family?"

"No. It's too dangerous to have any connection to me because of the job. I send them money through Den Mother. A shifter doc developed a reconstructive surgery, and if my sister has that operation, she may be able to walk."

Casey frowned. "You were going to use the money from killing me for the surgery."

Hunter speared him with a piercing look. "There will always be other jobs."

***

As they boarded the private jet, Rex greeted them. Hunter exchanged a fist bump with him. Casey explored the main passenger area.

"Wow, this is awesome!" When his foraging scored a container of premium mixed nuts, Little Wolf did a victory dance.

"First plane ride," he said to his buddy, and they exchanged a smile.

"Ah, should be in style, then." Akio had pulled out all the stops for this mission, sending the plane reserved for his wealthiest human clients.

Hunter took a seat next to Rex and accepted a beer. He leaned back and assumed a casual pose. He'd often visited swanky joints and traveled like the filthy rich for his job, but he'd never truly fit in. In some ways, he was still that young punk from Detroit, struggling to care for his family.

Once they were in the air, Casey roamed the cabin again. He'd discovered the bathroom and had been gone for fifteen minutes.

Rex chuckled as the toilet flushed for like the twentieth time. "He's a real kick in the pants."

"Yeah."

"He sure hit the pack lottery. Who knew our princess would turn out to be an actual prince?"

"Sure, it's just great." *A prince and a hit man, what a combo....*

"So, have you told him yet?" His friend fiddled with the label on his beer.

"Told him what?"

The other man frowned. "That you're mates, idiot."

He rubbed the back of his neck. "No. He's got a lot to deal with at the moment, and I'm not even sure we are."

Rex rolled his eyes. "If you're meant to be, you're meant to be. Can't fuck with fate."

Fate. What the fuck ever. But to be with Casey.... He didn't get all deep and shit, but suddenly, he wanted to be more. Popping bad guys had its place, but what if he could be the kind of man Casey deserved? Something small and fragile rose up in his chest. Hope. Been a really long time since he'd experienced that emotion.

He downed his beer. He hadn't heard any sound coming from the bathroom in a while, and Little Wolf hadn't returned. "Better check and make sure he didn't fall in."

The other shifter snorted. "He is an adult, you know."

Oh, yeah, he got that.

He knocked on the lavatory door. "Baby, you okay? You feeling sick?"

"I'm not in there, Hunter."

He swung around at his voice. "Where are you?"

Little Wolf laughed. "In the bedroom."

He slid open the door to find Casey spread out nude on a bed. He leisurely stroked his rigid cock, his eyes half-lidded.

Hunter froze, dumbstruck at the stunning sight in front of him. Jesus, how Casey could go from adorable to full-on sex god was a complete mystery, but he wasn't going to hurt his brain pondering it.

He closed the door behind him and crossed his arms over his chest. Sunlight from the window danced across the smaller man's golden skin, highlighting the splash of freckles on his shoulders and the rosy buds that stood out proud on a well-defined chest flushed pink with need. His gaze followed the ginger treasure trail leading to the main event.

"What are you up to, Little Wolf?"

"Well, since it's my first plane ride I figured I should join the Mile High Club. You wanna initiate me?" Casey gave him a sexy pout.

Fuck, yes. But for some perverse reason, Hunter wanted to toy with him a little first. "So, what did you have in mind?" He said it all casual and shit while his heart pounded out a freaking tribal beat.

The other man smiled, continuing to stroke his cock. "Well, Big Bad Wolf, maybe you could huff and puff and blow my cock down."

He suppressed a grin and raised an eyebrow, watching Casey palm his balls, his bent legs revealing his pink pucker. He ran his thumb over the tip and moaned.

Jesus, Hunter was so hard, his dick could have pounded through concrete.

Casey drew in a deep breath and released it. "What big eyes you have, Mr. Wolf."

"Better to watch you diddle yourself with, Little Wolf."

He yanked his shirt over his head and tossed it on the floor. Kicking off his shoes, he pulled off his socks.

Little Wolf sucked a finger into his mouth before running it around his hole. Hunter eye-fucked that delicious temptation, his upper lip curling over elongated fangs. Shit, he hoped that didn't freak the inexperienced shifter out.

"My, what big teeth you have," Casey said with a smile nearly as toothy.

"Better to eat you up with, baby."

The smaller man chuckled and then gasped as he impaled his entrance with one finger. Hunter's cock ached, and he rubbed it through his pants. Needing relief, he unfastened his jeans and yanked them down his legs before stepping out of them.

"What a big dick you have," Casey practically purred as he fucked himself with that single digit. *Lucky finger*.

Hunter grabbed his throbbing member and waved it enticingly in his direction. Two could play this game. "What do you want me to do with this big dick? Put it in that pretty little mouth of yours?"

"I want you to fuck me with it." The other were's voice dropped an octave or two. Damn, that raspy tone was sexy.

He fronted an arrogant expression and used his best trash-talking tone, "Think you can take it? It's much bigger than that little-bitty finger of yours."

The smaller shifter's eyes darkened at the

challenge. "Oh, yes, Mr. Wolf, I can take it. Every. Single. Inch."

Fuuuccckkk.

He slid onto the bed and palmed Casey's face, running his thumbs over those lightly freckled cheeks. Hunter stared into his beautiful blue eyes. Suddenly, it hit him. Mate or no, he loved Casey. His wolf agreed.

Adore. Love. Keep him?

He wanted nothing more to hold onto Little Wolf for the rest of his life. But he had things to do first. Mikaela and Mom needed him. For now, he'd focus on the sweet man before him and treasure whatever stolen time he had left.

He leaned over and captured Casey's lips, moaning as their tongues swirled together. They shared long, wet kisses. Hunter pulled back and grazed his teeth along the smaller man's jaw then moved on to suck and nibble an earlobe. Gasping, Casey dug his fingers in his biceps as Hunter nipped where his neck and shoulder met. He backed off quickly, his wolf too close to the surface.

He ran his hands over the other man's smooth chest and followed with his mouth, kissing his birthmark before tonguing and sucking his hard little nipples. The sounds Casey made were driving him crazy. He licked his abs before sliding his lips down the young were's flat stomach and engulfing his dick in his mouth.

"Uh!" Casey gripped the sheets and bucked up, making Hunter's eyes water. Hunter pressed down on the other man's hips to hold him steady and bobbed his head. He hummed in appreciation. Lord, Casey tasted good. He released his tasty treat and fisted the young were while cupping his balls, prolonging his pleasure.

"Hunter, please. Want to come with you inside me." Casey lobbed a small bottle of lube and a strip of condoms down the bed toward him. Little Wolf had scored more than mixed nuts from the plane's cubbyholes.

"Thanks, but shifters don't need to use condoms."

Casey's eyes widened. "Really?"

"Yeah, 'member how I mentioned we don't get diseases like humans do? That means STDs, too." He grinned. He loved schooling him on that particular factoid of shifter sex.

The smaller shifter's mouth gaped. "So, I can feel you...bare? I never...you...."

He chuckled. As Casey completely lost the ability to speak, Little Wolf's cheeks flushed and his eyes glazed over.

Hunter guided him into turning over, and the other man rose onto his hands and knees. He stroked his hands down the pale back all the way to those lean hips. He bent down and kissed the dimples at the top of his ass and nipped at one round cheek. Jesus, his Little Wolf truly had the sweetest bubble butt.

Casey gave a breathy laugh and pushed his ass up higher.

"Horny, much?" he growled.

The little shifter peered over his shoulder, his face tight with need. "Only for you."

The look, the words seared through him. *Mine.* His wolf preened.

He grasped his hips again, and Casey widened

his knees out, his pucker exposed to Hunter's view. He'd never rimmed anyone before. The act had seemed kind of nasty. Putting your dick in there— fine. But your tongue? *Fuck that noise.* The little pink hole fluttered, calling to him like a fucking Siren. Hunter ran his nose down his crease, inhaling his wonderful musky scent. Holding the cheeks apart, he experimentally flicked out his tongue, giving a tentative lick. The other man's hips shot forward as if he'd been electrocuted.

"Hunter!" He gasped and pushed his ass back toward Hunter's face with a wiggle.

Oh, Little Wolf liked that. He smirked then unleashed his tongue and mouth on that yummy ass. Flattening his tongue, he speared the tip in. He loved the wild sounds the other were made as he fucked him with his tongue.

He pulled back, flicked open the bottle, and lubed up his fingers. Reaching around, he fisted Casey's cock while inserting a finger and then two into his tight hole. He moaned as Hunter stretched him, preparing him.

"I need you so bad. Make me yours."

He squeezed his eyes shut, Casey's words running like a freight train through his body. Damn, he wanted to claim Little Wolf as his mate so fucking bad. He slicked up.

"Fuck, yeah." He pressed in, mesmerized as the head popped past the protective muscle. Hunter paused before letting his cock glide in. He groaned. *God, so tight.* Holding onto the other shifter's hips, he slowly sank in balls deep. Home, he was fucking home.

He retreated and slid back in at a slow, easy

pace. Casey's hot channel held him tight as a glove. *So hot. So good.* He needed this to be incredible for his Little Wolf. Sweat dripped down his face, and his muscles ached under the strain of holding back.

"Harder," Casey moaned. "Fuck me, Hunter."

He grunted and surged forward at a different angle. He knew he'd hit the right spot when the other man cried out, "Oh, yes!"

He continued to make incoherent sounds while Hunter pumped, nearing release. He shoved down his wolf who wailed to bite, to claim his mate. Instead, he reached around and stroked Casey while he pounded his flawless ass.

Little Wolf yelled as he came.

He swore and tensed. Casey's convulsing channel milked his cock. Gripping his hips hard, he yelled out as he exploded, releasing his seed deep inside him. A primal surge of pride and satisfaction coursed through him. He rested his face against the back of Little Wolf's neck and then kissed his shoulder before pulling out. His wolf rumbled happily when cum trickled down the back of his lover's muscular thigh.

He pulled him into a crushing embrace.

"Whoa, can't breathe." Casey chuckled.

Hunter let up and kissed him. It took all his control to release him.

Blue eyes twinkled up at him. "Best plane trip ever."

He huffed out a laugh and smiled. "Crazy Little Wolf."

Chapter Eight

"Ah, there you are! I was starting to think I needed to send in a rescue team. Who knew airplane toilets could be so treacherous," Rex said when they returned to the main cabin.

Casey smiled, his brain still blown by the most amazing sexual experience of his life.

"Why are you in a suit?" Hunter grabbed a couple bottled waters from the mini fridge and handed one over to him.

"There's been a change of plans, which requires us to suit up." Rex held out a garment bag.

Hunter took it from him. "What's up?"

"We're having dinner at Viktor Ivanov's Lake Minnetonka house. Pawlak and his beta will be there."

Hunter whistled. "Den Mother has some serious connections."

"Should I change, too?" He glanced at his button-down shirt and jeans.

"You're fine. We have to represent the organization as bodyguards."

Hunter slid past him to the back of the plane. Casey sat down and petted Priss, half listening to the other man as he talked about pack hierarchy. He was going to meet his father. What if he hated Casey? He didn't know squat about being a wolf....

"Hey, it's going to be okay," Rex said. Gone was the usual easygoing expression, and his eyes were intense. "If you don't like what's in Minnesota, you're outta there. And if things get hairy, Hunter's got your back." Rex paused. "We both do."

Casey smiled at him. "Thanks. You're a good egg."

The other man's face tightened, his eyes darkening, but before Casey could ask what was wrong, he was back to full-on asshat mode. "Yeah, well, don't be spreading that shit around. I've got a rep to uphold."

"Because look how far being an asshole has gotten you," Hunter said as he strode back in.

"True, that. I'm stuck with your sorry ass."

The big guy looked amazing in about anything and, damn, if he didn't rock a suit. Casey walked over to him and ran his hands over the lapels. Needing to touch the sexy man, he straightened his tie.

He stared up into somber dark brown eyes, and his chest constricted, reality hitting him over the head. He loved him. He loved Hunter. *Oh, shit.*

"Baby, if you keep looking at me like that, I'll have to take you back to the bedroom for a repeat performance."

He gulped and forced a smile on his face as he internally wigged out. He'd fallen in love with a man he couldn't ever expect to hold onto.

Rex laughed. "If I found my mate—man, I

wouldn't let him out the bedroom. We'd be fucking like bunnies 24/7."

But Hunter couldn't be his man. His stomach roiled, but he didn't regret what they'd shared. He'd just have to be strong enough to let him go. He stepped away from the large man and reclaimed his seat. Priss whined softly.

"You okay?" Concern filled Hunter's eyes.

He diverted his attention to Rex. "I'm fine. Say, are there other types of shifters, like bunnies?"

That set the other man off on a long list of shifters that had him reeling for a very different reason. So many kinds, and he hadn't known.

"There aren't any bunny shifters that I know of. But if there were, I'd be willing to fuck one," Rex said in a contemplative tone.

Hunter snorted. "Yeah, that would go well. After you were done fucking the dude into the mattress, your wolf would have him as a snack. Straight up the shortest hookup ever."

"Hmm, you may have a point there."

Casey rolled his eyes.

***

A limo waited on the tarmac as they disembarked. *Wow, another first.*

Once in the limo, Casey fidgeted and pushed all the buttons he could reach. The privacy partition went down and up. The Beastie Boys' "Fight for Your Right" blared out of the speakers. He winced, turned down the volume some, and then rapped along, doing a little head banging and air guitar action during the riffs. His wolf howled along, having a great time.

When Hunter laughed, he peered over at him. "What?"

The big guy shook his head and said with a grin, "White boys."

The limo entered a gated community and parked in front of a beautiful home, the biggest, most expensive place he'd ever seen.

"We're not in Kansas anymore, Priss," he whispered as the limo driver opened his door.

A butler-looking dude greeted them. "Come this way. The Ivanovs are looking forward to meeting you."

They followed him to a plush yet comfy living room with rich leather furniture. He wished it was cold enough to have a fire going in the ornate fireplace. A dark-haired bear of a man stood by a huge window with an amazing view of the backyard and lake.

"Hello, I'm Viktor Ivanov. Welcome to my home," he said with a thick Russian accent. He shook hands first with Casey and then Hunter and Rex. His grip was firm, his ice-blue eyes piercing. This man would be a fierce friend and an even fiercer enemy.

A statuesque woman with silvery blonde hair strode into the room, the picture of radiant elegance.

"Liliya, let me introduce you to—"

"Bazyli! We were overjoyed to learn you're alive." She rushed over and kissed both his cheeks before embracing him. She released him but held onto his hands.

He gave her a shy smile. "Nice to meet you. I go by Casey." At his feet, Priss yipped and danced in a circle. "And this is Priss."

Liliya smiled and bent down to pet him. "Your

mother, Krystiana, and I were very good friends. You have her eyes, you know."

"Come, let's sit," Viktor said.

They sat down, and Hunter and Rex stood off to the side, looking like scary-ass bodyguards with their suits and shades. He was glad they were with him.

"You've grown into such a handsome young man. To think I used to change your diapers. I called you Little Fountain because one had to watch out once that diaper came off," Liliya said.

He blushed as everyone chuckled.

"Casey, will you share with us where you've been?" Viktor said.

"I was raised in Eugene, Oregon, by my adopted mom, Maggie. She died last year. Cancer. I didn't know anything about my shifter family until now."

"Maggie?" Liliya's eyebrows rose. She stood and selected a photo album from a bookshelf. After leafing through it, she held it out to him.

She pointed to the people in the picture. "Here is our Anna, you, your mother, and Maggie."

He stared at the picture. Everyone had big smiles on their faces including *his* Maggie. "You knew her?"

"Yes, she was your nanny, and your father's before you."

"But she was human."

"Her family served the Pawlak family for centuries," Liliya said. "She was one of the most trusted people in the Pawlak household."

"She was a wonderful mom and kept me safe. I just don't understand why someone would want to kill me."

"You are the son of a powerful Alpha. Unfortunately, that makes you a target," Viktor said.

So, who else knows I'm alive?

Chapter Nine

Casey walked Priss in the backyard, hoping to burn off some nervous energy. He had a lot to process, and he hadn't even met his father yet. Hunter followed close behind, a silent sentinel.

He paused and touched his ear, listening to Rex, most likely. "Your father's arrived. I need to get in position. Don't mention what happened at the Market and keep personal details to a minimum until we figure out who's gunning for you."

He leaned up and gave the big wolf a quick peck of a kiss. "For luck."

Hunter held his face and more thoroughly kissed him. Flashing a wolfish grin, he strode up the lawn.

Liliya passed the large shifter as he returned to the house. She fanned herself when she reached Casey. "Krystiana and I used to dream of you and Anna getting married one day, but I think your devoted bodyguard is a perfect match for you."

He smiled and offered her his arm. *Showtime.*

Viktor led Aleksander and Marek out to the deck. His father looked older than the picture he'd seen, his hair more silver than blond, and he had bags under his eyes. His pallor was in stark contrast to his beta's tanned skin. Black haired with flashing green eyes, Marek was handsome in a rakish kind of way.

"Alek and Marek, I'd like you to meet Casey Smith, our other guest this evening," Liliya said.

His father leaned in to shake his hand then turned as pale as a ghost. Marek grabbed his elbow, but Alek shook him off and hugged Casey tightly.

Jeez, wolves really don't believe in personal space, do they?

"Bazyli, how can this be?" His father collapsed into the chair Marek pulled out for him.

"Alpha Pawlak, I think you got too much sun from golfing earlier," Marek said.

His father glared at Marek. "Do you think a father would forget his own child's scent? This is Bazyli, I tell you."

Liliya spoke up, "Perhaps you could show them your birthmark, Casey."

He unbuttoned his shirt enough to reveal the crescent moon.

"See, my son! But how can this be? You died in the fire."

Everyone took seats near his father, and drinks were served. He was sandwiched between his father and Marek. Marek's scent had an odd, sickening undertone, like rotten meat. His wolf gagged, and he tried to breathe shallowly.

"I was with Maggie. She thought everyone died in the fire, so she raised me around humans," he said as he fixed his shirt.

"So many lost years," his father said and then clapped his hands together. "But, now, we are reunited, and that is all that matters."

"How did you get here, Casey?" Marek asked.

"Before Maggie died, she said if I needed any help I should contact Liliya." He gave an aww shucks shrug. "I ran into a cash flow problem, so figured it couldn't hurt."

"Viktor flew him out on his private jet," Liliya said.

"Of course, he did." Marek's smile bordered on a sneer.

"Well, money will never be an issue again." His father nodded. "You are my heir and successor."

"But, Alpha Pawlak, he wasn't raised with the pack. How will he know how to lead?"

"He will marry a strong partner to assist him in the ways, of course! There are several suitable young ladies who would love to marry our Baz—Casey," his father said and started listing off girls' names and the packs they belonged to.

He'd just met his father, and he was already trying to marry him off—and to the wrong team, no less. He wished Priss was out here instead of in the house. His wolf paced, on edge. He'd never been in the closet, and he wasn't about to jump in now.

"Uh, sir, I'm gay."

Alek paused and stared at him for a moment. "Oh, well I'm sure we can find you a proper male partner as well. What about that handsome young man from the Miami pack, Jackson something?"

Marek made a weird preening gesture. "Or he could marry me. I know all about the Pawlak pack and could help ease his transition."

His stomach turned. How could he marry this horrible-smelling man who was at least double his age?

"Oh, that's a marvelous idea, Marek!"

No effing way. He gulped. "Sir, I don't think—"

"There would be a long engagement, of course." His father continued as if he hadn't spoken. "So you have time to truly get to know it each other."

Marek leered, running his hand down Casey's arm. "Yes, I'd like to know you properly."

Bile rose in his throat, and his wolf prepared to bolt.

"Alek, arranged marriages are so old fashioned." Liliya waved her hand in the air. "Perhaps you should let him choose. Maybe he'll find his mate."

Mate?

Marek scowled. "Men don't have male mates."

His father raised a hand. "Liliya has a point. Casey will find the person best suited to help him lead the pack."

"Sir, I've never wanted to be a leader."

"Some of our best leaders never aspired to lead, but stepped up when they were called upon to do so," Viktor said.

Air, he needed air.

He took a deep cleansing breath and choked on Marek's foul stench. "I don't think I can do this. Maybe I should just go home."

"Oh, Casey, why would you want to go back to Oregon when you can have everything you'd ever need right here?" Marek caressed the back of his neck.

He stifled a shudder of revulsion and stiffened. "I never mentioned Oregon."

Marek's hand tightened. "You didn't? I'm sure you did—"

"No, he didn't," Viktor said, his eyes cold.

"You're hurting me."

"Marek, let him go. What's going on?" His father protested, slamming his fist on the table.

Marek stood and yanked him up out of his chair by his hair, a knife pressed against his throat.

Rex emerged from the house, his gun drawn and trained on Marek. "Let him go now and maybe we'll let you live."

Marek used Casey's body as a shield and snarled, "I had plans, and you've ruined everything."

"What do you mean?" his father demanded.

"I was the youngest beta in our pack's history and destined to be the next pack leader until that bitch popped that mewling baby out of her cunt."

"Marek, you will not speak of my mate in such a disgusting manner."

Marek laughed, and the knife jabbed Casey harder, drawing blood. He slowed his breathing, trying to stay calm. He needed to keep it together.

"I drugged dinner that night. Poor Mommy was unconscious on the nursery floor. It would have been so easy to smother the little brat in his crib."

Everyone gasped.

"But that bitch Maggie knocked me out with a fire poker and escaped with the whelp. I started the fire as I'd planned and waited for little Bazyli to return."

He tried to slump, making the beta a bigger target, but Marek's grip tightened, preventing movement.

"No word of Bazyli, but I couldn't rest until I'd found you, destroyed you. And where had you been hiding? In Oregon, working as a fucking potter!"

Marek spat and moved toward the deck stairs, yanking him along. "Now I get to kill you, after all."

A shot rang out, and Marek fell, dragging Casey down with him. Rex stalked over and kicked the knife away.

"Confirmed dead. Send in a cleanup crew." The large man's voice sounded over the roaring of his heartbeat.

Rex helped him stand, and he started to shake. Wrapping his arms around himself, he walked a few steps before sinking to the deck, the smell of blood making him nauseous. He dry heaved.

Liliya dropped to her knees and pulled him against her chest. He turned his face into her comforting warmth. "Viktor, get him a drink."

A glass was thrust into his hands. He obediently drank and coughed, hard alcohol burning his throat. Liliya rubbed his back and stood.

The smell of apple cider and rain hit his nostrils, calming him. *Hunter.* He blinked up as his lover strode toward him, leading Priss. A giggle broke loose at the contrast of the big, powerful man, his rifle slung over a shoulder, walking a tiny dog.

Priss jerked loose and ran up to him, whining. "It's okay, Priss. I'm fine." His voice was rough and shaky.

Casey reached for him, but Priss dodged him and ran over to Marek's body, barking fiercely. The dog grabbed one of Marek's pant cuffs with his teeth and shook his head, growling.

"Miss Priscilla! Stop that!" Priss ran back to him, and he hugged the animal close. "Naughty boy."

Rex laughed. "I love that dog."

Hunter passed his rifle over to his friend and

bent down, scooping both him and Priss up. "Let's get you in the house, Little Wolf."

Damn, the big shifter was strong.

"No, I can walk." He squirmed. They might call him a princess, but he was no damsel.

"Shush. Let me do this." Hunter tightened his hold, and he settled back, soaking in the powerful man's scent.

Hunter kissed his temple after he placed him on the couch. Liliya sat down next to him. "I need to talk to your father. Will you be okay with Liliya?"

He nodded, and Hunter lightly brushed the small puncture wound on his neck. "So brave, Little Wolf."

Chapter Ten

Hunter sat across from Casey's father in Viktor's private den. Wasn't this a fucked-up way to meet the 'rent?

"Thank you for saving my son. Viktor and I will send signed statements that this was a justified killing to the Council, so you are free to go without pack recourse. However, I would be honored if you'd join my pack."

"I appreciate the offer, sir, but I have obligations to my family."

Alek sighed. "Casey will need protection in case Marek's poison has spread to others in our pack."

"My boss is sending a few men I'd trust with my life. The Ivanovs have invited him to stay here until they arrive."

"Are you sure you won't stay? If money is an issue, I can cover whatever you need. Viktor told me Marek had offered two million for his life. I'm willing to give you four million to stay."

He squinted. Damn, the Alpha was playing hardball. "Sir, that's a very generous offer, but I can't take your money."

"Why not? Don't you want to be with him?"

"More than anything, but I won't let money come between us. I need to do this on my terms."

"I respect that. My son is lucky to have a mate like you."

His glance shot up to meet the Alpha's sharp eyes. "Take good care of him. He doesn't know much about shifters, and I haven't told him we're mates."

"I will do my very best. Return to my son soon. It will be hard for you to be separated, even without the bond." Alex offered his hand, and they shook.

Hunter returned to the living room, and Liliya left to give them privacy.

"I already said goodbye to Rex. He left with the cleanup crew. So, I guess it's time for you to go," Casey said, his voice tight.

"Yes, I wish—"

"I know you have your family to look after." Casey's Adam's apple bobbed. "I'm going to miss you, Hunter."

He clenched his jaw, wishing he could make promises about coming back, wishing he could tell Casey he loved him, but he couldn't do either until he was out of the gun-for-hire business. But there was one thing he could leave him with. "Jamal. My real name is Jamal," he said and drew the little shifter into him.

"I'll miss you, Jamal," Casey said against his chest.

It'd been a long time since he'd heard his own name. And to hear it from Casey.... *Suck it up, man. Don't you dare cry like a bitch.* "I'm going to miss you too, Little Wolf."

His wolf howled in pain.

He tightened his hold for a moment and kissed the top of his lover's head, inhaling his scent one last time. He released the smaller man. "If you need anything, contact Den Mother. Akio will help. Stay safe."

Casey nodded and sniffled. "You stay safe, too. Good luck to your sister."

He bent down and gave Priss some love. "Take care of him, little man."

Priss yipped and pawed at him.

His chest aching, Hunter stood and strode out of the room, out of the house to the back lawn, and climbed into the awaiting chopper.

Chapter Eleven

With Akio's assistance, Casey Smith died and Casey Pawlak was born. His father insisted he have at least one bodyguard around even though the danger had most likely died with Marek.

He was adjusting to living in the huge Alpha house. Father really tried to make him feel at home. He'd even set up a studio and pottery kiln for him.

Living in northern Minnesota rocked. He and his wolf loved running in the woods. After all the years of suppressing his wolf nature, it was so freeing to finally embrace it. He and his father were slowly building a solid relationship; having Maggie as a common connection had really helped.

He concentrated on getting to know his new pack and staying busy. It was hard not to miss Hunter. Priss covered his ears with his paws when Casey sang along to sad songs. His wolf howled, as emo as a lovesick schoolgirl.

"Casey, are you listening?" his father asked one night while they played chess in his study a few weeks after he'd moved in.

"Sorry, my mind drifted."

His father gave him a knowing look. "Missing your Hunter, are you?"

He grimaced. "Not sure he could be called *my* Hunter."

"I offered him four million dollars to stay."

"You did? What did he say?"

"He thanked me but said he couldn't take my money. He couldn't let it come between you. And he was right. You would always wonder if he was here because of the money or because of you."

"At least he'd be here," he grumbled.

"He's your mate. He would be here if he could."

"I heard that term before. Is it like a soul mate?"

"Finding one's mate is a rare and precious thing. The attraction is very strong, and once shifters are mated, their bond can only be broken by death." He gave a sad smile.

"How do they bond?"

His father pulled his shirt collar away from his neck. "With a bite, leaving the bonding mark." He stared at the faint scars, puncture marks of a wolf's bite. His breath hitched at the thought of Hunter biting him in this manner. But he hadn't, had he?

He poked his lip out. "But if we're mates, why didn't he bite me?"

"Once wolves are bonded, it is impossible for them to be apart for long. Even now, it is difficult for him to be separated from you. And it's why you're feeling the way you do."

"But Marek said—"

"I've learned most of what came from that monster's mouth was lies. I have no doubt Hunter is your mate."

"So, he'll come back?"

"Yes." His father moved a pawn.

He and his wolf hoped his father was right.

"Dad, how did you manage after Mom died? Since you were bonded?"

His father sighed and rose. He stood with him. "I was devastated. A part of me died with her. And losing you both, I came close to giving up. I'm so glad I didn't. Having you here has brought me great joy."

Casey hugged him.

***

Casey stared at his reflection in the full-length mirror in his bedroom. The suit Rex had bought him fit amazingly well without tailoring, like it'd been made for him. He wasn't in the mood to party, but his father had honored his wishes to delay his homecoming party for months already. He knew this was important to his father, and he wanted him to be happy. At least one of them would be.

"Ready to go, Priss?"

The little dog yapped and trotted over, looking dapper with his sparkly collar on. Casey scooped him up and snuggled his face into his fur. Thank God he had Priss.

He went downstairs, pausing to talk to a few guests. He kissed Liliya's cheeks. She had become a wonderful friend, helping him navigate the strange world of pack politics. Having her here centered him.

"Hopefully, there'll be less excitement at this dinner party than the last one," he said, finally relaxing some.

Liliya laughed and winked. "Well, maybe some

excitement is good."

He opened his mouth to ask her what she meant when the faint scent of smoke, rain, and apple cider hit him. His nostrils flared, and his heart rate jacked up. "Hunter."

His wolf reared up. *Mate.*

He spun around and scanned the room, frantic to find his other half.

There he was, toward the back of room, looking absolutely amazing in an expensive suit, tailored to showcase his tall, powerful body. "Excuse me, Liliya. I have to go."

"Let me take Priss for you," she said, and he handed over the leash and was on the move. Somehow, he managed to navigate the room without running into anyone, his sole focus on the man he loved. He stopped in front of him, trying to breathe normally. Hunter's expression was neutral as he gave Casey a heated once over.

"Looking good, Little Wolf." His voice was low and deep.

"You, too," he said, sounding hoarse to his own ears.

"So, this is quite a party." The large man glanced around.

"I'm glad you're here. I didn't know you were coming." He intended to have a word with his father in the very near future.

"Wasn't sure I was going to make it."

"How are you?"

"Good. My sister had her surgery a few weeks ago. She can walk and shift now."

"That's awesome news!"

"Was good to see her and Mom again."

His breath caught. "Does that mean you're done with the job?"

"Officially retired."

Damn, the man's face didn't give anything away. His chest tightened as he stared into dark chocolate eyes.

"So, do I call you Hunter or Jamal?

"Sorry I forgot to introduce myself. Hello, my name is Jamal Hunter."

"Aren't you the clever man?" He laughed.

The big guy grinned. "I thought so."

"What do you plan to do now?"

"Depends on you."

"On me?"

"Do you have room in your life for a retired assassin?"

His eyes welled. "Yes, I do."

He placed his hands on Hunter's muscular chest and peered up at him, suddenly shy.

The large man dipped his head and kissed him, long and deep. God, he'd missed those kisses. He intertwined a leg with Hunter's and darted his tongue into his mouth. *Yummy.*

His big wolf pulled back, breathing hard. "We keep this up, and we're going to give your guests an eyeful."

"Should we move to my room?"

"Fuck, yes."

Chapter Twelve

Casey yanked at his tie. Why did he have to be wearing so many damn clothes?

"Here, let me help you before you strangle yourself," Hunter said, sweeping Casey's fingers away.

He sighed with relief as the knot loosened. Hunter slid the tie from his neck and set it on top of his discarded suit jacket and returned to unbuttoning his own dress shirt.

He stilled, his full attention on the muscular body being revealed one button at a time. God, Hunter was so beautiful. He pushed the shirt off his mate's shoulders and ran his hands down his arms before exploring his chest. Casey kissed and nibbled taut espresso skin as he undid the other man's pants. He needed to taste Hunter like he needed air. No one had ever tasted so good. He started to drop to his knees, but the big guy grabbed him by the elbows and hauled him back up.

"As much as I'd love to fuck that sweet mouth of yours, I need to be inside you," Hunter said.

He loved that his bad-ass mate sounded on edge.

He stripped off the rest of his clothes and slung his arms around Hunter's neck, pouring his soul into his kiss. The large shifter palmed his butt, lifting him. He hopped up, encasing his lover's waist with his legs. Groaning, he rubbed his cock against Hunter's stomach as they kissed. His mate marched over to the bed and sat down.

Balancing on hard, muscled thighs, he shivered as Hunter's strong hands mapped out his body while their tongues danced. Panting, he grasped his arms for leverage and slid his butt along his mate's erection. He gasped, feeling it brush against his hole.

"Lube?"

"In the drawer." He waved toward his nightstand and giggled as the big wolf leaned over, his long arm reaching out. He took the opportunity to nibble on his mate's ear.

Hand digging around in the drawer, Hunter growled triumphantly when he found the lube. He bit down on his earlobe then licked away the sting.

His mate moaned, and Casey heard the snick of the lube bottle.

Moist fingers prepared him as they continued to kiss. Casey rode those fingers, keening with pleasure.

"Jesus, baby, the sounds you make. I love it," the big guy rasped and moved to slick up.

He rose up hovering over the head of Hunter's cock and slowly pressed down. The head breached his entrance, and he moaned at the slight burn as he stretched to take his mate's big dick. *So good.*

He stared into Hunter's face while he slid down, taking in every inch. The man's brows bunched together, and his jaw clenched when Casey bottomed out with a gasp. He was so full, his mate so impossibly deep inside him. Hunter held his hips, letting him get used to the intense position, but he needed to move. With shallow movements, he fucked himself on Hunter's cock. The large man groaned and pushed up to meet him on his downward trek. Soon, he was rising and slamming down on that massive cock.

Feeling close to exploding, he leaned his head against his mate's shoulder as he pumped into him. Rubbing his face into the crook of Hunter's neck, he grazed his skin with his teeth. Suddenly, the need to bite his mate hammered through him. But he didn't want to hurt Hunter....

The big shifter groaned and dropped his head to Casey's shoulder. "Yes, Mate. Do it."

With Hunter's teeth on him, his canines lengthened and clamped down. The powerful wolf's teeth piercing his skin and the taste of his mate's blood sent him spiraling out of control. He came, shooting ribbons of cum against Hunter's stomach. His mate shouted, and his dick pulsed, filling Casey with his release.

Hunter licked his shoulder. The burn instantly soothed. He followed his example, his mate's wound immediately sealed.

They moved up onto the bed, stretching out.

"I love you, Casey."

He snuggled against Hunter's chest. "I love you too, my mate."

"Don't get too comfortable. We need to go back downstairs. Your dad will kill me if we miss dinner."

"Don't want to go. Want to stay with you in bed."

Hunter kissed his mark. "I do, too, but remember, we have forever now."

Forever. He smiled.

"Do you think your family would like to come live with us?"

"Yeah, I'm sure they would," Hunter husked out, his dark eyes gleaming.

Casey leaned up and kissed him. "Perfect."

His mate returned the kiss before popping him on the butt. "Now, let's get out of this bed before I lose my resolve."

They quickly dressed and rejoined the party, making it just in time to be seated for dinner.

His dad stood. "Thank you all for coming and welcoming my son, Casey Pawlak, who has brought so much joy to me and the pack. Please also welcome his mate, Jamal Hunter, the man who returned Casey to us."

Everyone clapped, and when they kissed, a wolf whistle rang out. He glanced out into the room. Rex sat with the Ivanovs. He smiled as their friend held up Priss' paw to wave at him.

***

Propped up on his elbow, Hunter stared down at his beautiful mate as he slept. Casey lay on his back, one arm flung over his head. He smiled. Little Wolf was worn out. They'd made slow, sweet love after the party. Their bond now amplified each caress, each kiss, their connection allowing them to sense each other's emotions.

Being apart from Casey had been so hard—Rex had called him a whiny pussy more than once—but he was glad Little Wolf had time to adjust to his new life. It'd been right to delay their bonding until he was ready. Now that they were bonded, Hunter wasn't going anywhere. He would focus on his adorable mate, his family, and their new pack. After all his travels, he was finally home.

He touched the bonding mark at the juncture of his neck and shoulder, feeling truly complete for the first time in his life.

His wolf whined. Poor guy hadn't had a chance to see his mate yet.

"Soon, Wolf. We'll go out and run together soon." But it wouldn't hurt to let his wolf loose for a little while.

He shifted, and his wolf huffed out a happy sigh.

Adore. Love. Keep!

He nuzzled the bonding mark on Casey's shoulder before burrowing his nose in his armpit, inhaling the musky scent of his mate.

The little shifter giggled and swatted at him. "Silly wolf, sleep not play."

Hunter's wolf licked his cheek and rested his large head on his mate's chest.

Casey sleepily stroked it. "Love you, too, Wolf."

Epilogue

Nicodemus glanced around and smiled. His audience had grown since he'd begun the story.

"Hunter's family came to live with them. When it was time for his father to step down as Alpha, Casey took his rightful place as leader of the Pawlak pack. He and his bond mate spent their days serving the people, and the pack thrived under their peaceful leadership.

"When not doing official pack business, Casey created pottery or worked in his garden. Hunter and his beta, Rex, ran an automotive repair shop. Each summer, they hosted an epic game of paintball assassins, and shifters came from far and wide to play.

"And they all lived happily ever after. The end."

The crowd clapped and drifted away, yet a young man lingered. He nervously brushed at his wispy multicolored hair, the palest white blond with splashes of black. He crinkled his little button nose, reminding Nicodemus of a wee rabbit.

"Did you have a question, lad?"

"Oh, no, it was a great story. I wish it were real."
He sighed and dropped a battered dollar into the hat.

"All good stories have at least an element of
truth, my boy," Nicodemus said with a wink.

About the Author

V.S. Morgan has lived all over the US but calls Minnesota her home now. She's been writing stories since she could hold a pencil and dreams of happily ever afters - even for two hot men - because love knows no boundaries. V.S. writes IRMC contemporary, paranormal, and suspense m/m and m/f with heart.

Also by V.S. Morgan

Rex's Mate
Sam's Temptation
The Gift